SCH 823.914 POW

Harry
the Superhero

Chris Powling
and Scoular Anderson

D0333119

YORK ST. JOHN
COLLEGE LIBRARY

WITHDRAWN

13 JUN 2022

York St. John College

3 8025 00482941 5

Look out for more *Jets* from Collins

Jessy Runs Away • *Best Friends* • **Rachel Anderson**

Ivana the Inventor • *Ernest the Heroic Lion Tamer* • **Damian Burnard**

Two Hoots • *Almost Goodbye Guzzler* • **Helen Cresswell**

Shadows on the Barn • **Sara Garland**

Nora Bone • *The Mystery of Lydia Dustbin's Diamonds* • **Brough Girling**

Thing on Two Legs • *Thing in a Box* • **Diana Hendry**

Desperate for a Dog • *More Dog Trouble* • **Rose Impey**

Georgie and the Dragon • *Georgie and the Planet Raider* • **Julia Jarman**

Cowardy Cowardy Cutlass • *Free With Every Pack* • **Robin Kingsland**

Mossop's Last Chance • *Mum's the Word* • **Michael Morpurgo**

Hiccup Harry • *Harry's Party* • *Harry with Spots On* • *Harry Moves House* •
Chris Powling

Rattle and Hum, Robot Detectives • **Frank Rodgers**

Our Toilet's Haunted • **John Talbot**

Rhyming Russell • *Messages* • **Pat Thomson**

Monty the Dog Who Wears Glasses • *Monty's Ups and Downs* • **Colin West**

Ging Gang Goolie, it's an Alien • *Stone the Crows, it's a Vacuum Cleaner* •
Bob Wilson

First published by A & C Black Ltd in 1995
Published by Collins in 1996
10 9 8 7 6 5
Collins is an imprint of HarperCollins*Publishers*Ltd,
77–85 Fulham Palace Road, Hammersmith, London W6 8JB

ISBN 0 00 675100-8

Text © 1995 Chris Powling
Illustrations © 1995 Scoular Anderson

The author and the illustrator assert the moral right
to be identified as the author and the illustrator of the work.
A CIP record for this title is available from the British Library.
Printed in Great Britain by
Clays Ltd, St Ives plc

All rights reserved. No part of this publication may be reproduced, stored in a retrieval
system, or transmitted in any form or by any means, electronic, mechanical, photocopying,
recording or otherwise, without the prior permission of HarperCollins*Publishers* Ltd,
77–85 Fulham Palace Road, Hammersmith, London W6 8JB.

I blame Batman.

Or maybe it was Superman's fault.

Come to think of it, Indiana Jones
wasn't much use either. Did they all
get together one day to nobble me?

I can guess how
it happened . . .

Superman was
the ring leader,
I expect.

That got them worried, I bet:
After all, who'd want to be an
out-of-work superhero?

See what I mean?

That's why they decided I was a
dangerous rival, I reckon. Once
Harry the Superhero started
righting wrongs, saving lives and
making the world a better place to
live in, they realised their
adventures would be over.

So, I'm convinced they kept away
from me on purpose.

How else could I have
got into such a mess?

Being a superhero myself, though,
I'm bound to escape eventually,
even if I can't manage it right at
this moment.

Besides, this little breather gives
me a chance to tell you how it all
began – like Superman flying so fast
he can turn time back on itself.

You don't think I can do it?

Just watch me . . . hold your breath,
cross your fingers and turn over
the page.

See?

It all started at school in a special assembly. Mrs Cadett, our headteacher, said,

Anyway, he told us about the Gre
Cross Code and keeping clear of
railway lines and watching out for
strangers who might want to
harm us.

He was terrific.

We'd heard it all before, but he
made it sound really important as
well as a bit scary.

14

15

I hadn't thought of that. What's more, Indiana Jones was bound to be lost in some deep, dark jungle on the other side of the world. This was serious.

Somehow, when it came to superheroes, our town had been left out.

Okay, so we didn't have many super-villians either (apart from Miss Hobbs), but that wasn't the point. Even when PC Motson went on to show us his whistle, his walkie-talkie, his handcuffs and his truncheon, I didn't feel any better.

And I'm sure his bicycle wasn't nearly as fast as the batmobile either.

The trouble was, nobody else saw the danger. When I tried to discuss it with Miss Hobbs, she gave me one of her looks.

The other kids were just as bad.

Funny?

What was funny about a shortage of superheroes? It could be disastrous couldn't it? Suppose a spacecraft full of aliens crash-landed in my back garden, for instance. PC Motson couldn't handcuff them all by himself.

That's when I had my brainwave . . .

I could see it so clearly, so vividly
in my mind's eye.

And I'd come zooming out of the blue to rescue them.

Brilliant.

There was only one problem that I could see. How do you become a superhero in the first place? When I asked Mrs Cadett she just laughed.

She'd be sorry when I was world famous and they'd renamed the school after me.

First, I went to the library to borrow everything I could – which wasn't very much. When I complained about this, the librarian wasn't very helpful. Actually, she seemed to be giggling.

Next I broke into my piggy-bank,

and spent a fortune hiring
video tapes. At least there were
plenty of those.

Best of all, though, was
remembering Grandad's
collection of ancient Beanos and
Dandys after I'd run out of money.

When I took some of these to the smelly old comic shop in the High Street, the shopkeeper was delighted.

There was so much material now, I had to veg out on it for hours up in my bedroom. It was all top-secret, of course, though I did let my little sister, Susie, in on it.

Gradually my project began to take shape. Here's what I discovered – sorted out into a handy action-plan. Feel free to copy it if you fancy a life of adventure yourself.

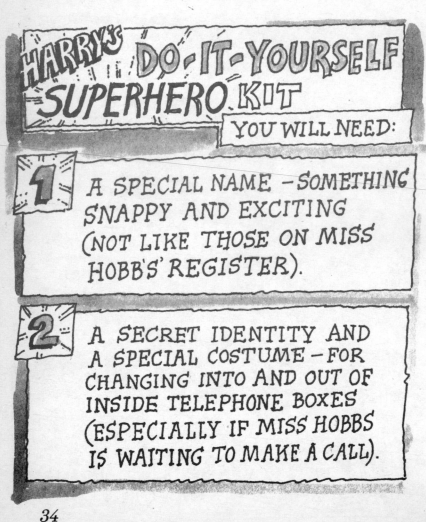

HARRY'S DO-IT-YOURSELF SUPERHERO KIT

YOU WILL NEED:

1 A SPECIAL NAME – SOMETHING SNAPPY AND EXCITING (NOT LIKE THOSE ON MISS HOBB'S REGISTER).

2 A SECRET IDENTITY AND A SPECIAL COSTUME – FOR CHANGING INTO AND OUT OF INSIDE TELEPHONE BOXES (ESPECIALLY IF MISS HOBBS IS WAITING TO MAKE A CALL).

3 A HIDE-OUT - PREFERABLY DARK, GLOOMY AND VAST ENOUGH TO STORE WEIRD EQUIPMENT (LIKE MISS HOBB'S STOCKROOM).

4 PRACTICE - AT FLYING, FIGHTING AND AMAZING FEATS OF DARING (LIKE ANSWERING MISS HOBBS BACK).

Of course, sorting out all these items at once won't be easy. Even I had a few disappointments.

Pretty soon, though, I was ready to take my rightful place amongst the world's living legends as . . .

INDIANA SUPERBAT

Well, at least my little sister was impressed.

Boolurg!

35

Naturally, there were one or two teething problems. Mum wasn't thrilled about the way I turned our kitchen into a gymnasium, for instance.

And Dad was completely useless as a super-villian when I asked him to help with my training programme.

The costume was tricky as well.
How did Batman carry his about,
I wonder?

I tried a
ruck-sack,

and
a suitcase.

But neither were very handy.

As for changing into it . . . well, I
hope Clark Kent found a phone box
a lot faster than I did. And I hope
there wasn't a man making him wait
while he described his whole life
story to someone at the other end.

It was incredibly cramped inside as well. What with bumping my knees and elbows on the sticking-out bits and people rapping on the glass all the time, I ended up a nervous wreck.

So I decided to speed things up by wearing my superhero outfit under my clothes.

Smart, eh?

Except, somehow, this didn't look right. I'm pretty sure people didn't point at Bruce Wayne and Clark Kent the way they did at me.

Never mind, I told myself, I was still practising, wasn't I? Once I'd performed a few daring rescues, they'd all be clapping not laughing.

Wrong again.

Even helping an old lady across the road turned out to be more difficult than I'd expected.

Honestly, she could have caused
an accident.

The kid whose kite I rescued wasn't very grateful, either.

Well, thank you.

I was so fed up I almost missed the
escaped black panther.

All right, so it was a wildcat. Okay, a kitten . . . but a scratchy, spitty kitten frightened silly from being trapped at the top of the tree. It belonged to a girl I know in the Infants.

She just looked at me with her eyes full of tears and her bottom lip trembly.

So I had to give it a go.

I was a little nervous, I admit. Especially when I got hold of the kitten – rather, the kitten got hold of me.

That's when I had my first flying lesson . . .

Thank goodness for one of those road-worker's tents which was pitched very handily.

Mind you, the workmen who happened to be inside when I landed, weren't too pleased.

I ask you, have any of the other superheroes ever had a clip round the ear?

By the time I got home I was in a real mood. Luckily, Mum and Susie were out shopping and Dad was in the greenhouse growing triffids.

I crept
upstairs to
my bedroom,
where I could
feel sorry for
myself in private.

That's when I heard the noises –
footsteps-on-the-roof type noises
and the lifting up of a skylight. Was
someone breaking into our attic?
Normally, I'd have been scared stiff,
but not after the sort of morning I'd
had. FURIOUS is what I was. A
burglar in the house of a superhero?

The cheek of it.

Of course, I made sure he knew
I was coming.

Even then, I think I expected them to back me up.

After this came a crash-bang-wallopy bit I'd rather forget.

That's why I'm upside-down beside
the water tank with a gag round my
mouth, and tape round my arms
and legs, while someone with a
flashlight looks through
Grandad's comics.

Grandad's comics? Who'd want to
steal those?

Daft, I call it.
Especially now
I could hear more
footsteps coming
up the stairs,
on dutyish footsteps,
with a whistle,
walkie-talkie,
handcuffs and
a truncheon
attached to them.

Well, he would have said that if
he'd been a comic-strip policeman
instead of the best home-beat
constable in the universe – a
supercop, you might say.

62

What a good thing he'd been on
patrol in our street just when Dad
spotted the burglar on the roof!
Later, I recognised who our burglar
was – the man who'd been hanging
about in the comic shop when I took
in my swops.

Did you spot him too?

Later still, when Dad and I visited
the comic shop, we realised why
Grandad's hoard was worth stealing.